Every new generation of children is enthralled by the famous stories in our Well-loved Tales series. Younger ones love to have the story read to them. Older children will enjoy the exciting stories in an easy-to-read text.

Published by Ladybird Books Ltd Loughborough Leicestershire UK
Ladybird Books Inc Lewiston Maine 04240 USA

The Brave Little Tailor

retold for easy reading
by ANNE McKIE

illustrated by KEN McKIE

Ladybird Books

Early one morning, a tailor was sitting at his window sewing a pair of trousers. He looked up from his work for a moment, and saw a country girl on her way to market. Her basket was full of jars of fresh fruit jam.

Now the tailor loved jam. It was almost breakfast time, so he bought some, and spread it on crusty bread ready to eat. First, however, he had to finish stitching the pair of trousers.

All at once, a swarm of flies flew down onto the tailor's bread and jam. This made him very cross. He grabbed a piece of cloth and took a great swipe at the flies.

To his surprise, he killed seven of them.
He was very pleased with himself. "How
wonderful I am!" he thought. "How
brave! The whole world must be told
about me."

He sat down straightaway and made himself a belt. Then he stitched the words SEVEN AT ONE BLOW on it in big letters.

"I will leave my shop, and tell the whole world how brave I am," he decided.

He picked up a little round cheese made of goat's milk to eat on his way, and locked his door behind him. As he set off, he noticed a tiny brown bird trapped in a bush. He freed it gently and popped it into his pocket.

Proudly he strode through the streets of
the town, shouting about his deed. People
were frightened when they heard him.

"Seven at one blow!" they whispered in wonder, then ran inside and locked their doors. No one knew that the seven he had killed were only flies.

The little tailor marched across the valley and up the hill. Suddenly, a great shadow fell across his path. It was an enormous giant.

"Get out of my way!" yelled the tailor, and he opened his coat and pointed to his belt.

The giant read the words "SEVEN AT ONE BLOW", and he gasped. Then he began to laugh. "We'll have a contest!" he roared. "If you win, I'll let you pass."

With that, he picked up a stone. He squeezed it with all his might, until one drop of water oozed out.

Quick as a flash, the tailor remembered the little round cheese in his pocket. He squeezed it with one hand until the water ran onto the ground. The giant was amazed, for he thought it was a stone.

Next the giant picked up another stone and threw it over the hill. They heard it fall with a mighty splash into the lake beyond.

As it fell, the tailor remembered the little brown bird in his pocket. He pretended it was a stone and threw it into the air. It flew straight up into the sky. "*Your* stone fell into the lake, but mine will *never* fall to earth!" boasted the little tailor.

"If you are as strong as that, help me to carry this tree," ordered the giant — and he pulled a great oak out of the ground.

"All right," replied the tailor. "You carry the trunk and I'll carry the branches, because there are more of them," he added craftily.

The tailor jumped up into the branches, where he was hidden by leaves. The poor giant ended up carrying both the tree and the clever little tailor as well.

The oak tree was so heavy the giant soon had to put it down. Then the tailor sprang out and lifted both his arms up to the branches, just as though he had been carrying the tree all the time.

The giant was so impressed that he invited the tailor to spend the night with him and his two huge brothers. For supper, each giant ate a whole roast sheep, and drank a whole barrel of wine.

After supper, they gave the tailor an enormous bed to sleep in. It was much too big for him, so he slept in a corner of the room instead.

The three giants were very worried about this tiny tailor who had killed SEVEN AT ONE BLOW. When they thought he was asleep, they crept up with

their heavy clubs in their hands and began
to beat the tailor's bed. They beat it so
hard that they broke it.

Since the tailor had been in his corner all the time, he was quite safe. So next morning he was up early, whistling and singing.

The three giants were so shocked that their terrible beating had failed to kill him that they ran away in fear. They were never seen again.

The brave little tailor marched all that day through towns and countryside, boasting of his deeds. "SEVEN AT ONE BLOW!" he would cry, showing off his belt.

After many miles he came to a palace.
He was so tired with travelling that he fell
asleep by the gate. When the soldiers of
the palace guard came by, they saw his
belt and the words "SEVEN AT ONE
BLOW". They rushed to tell the king.

The king sent a soldier to wake him up and bring him into the palace, for he believed that the tailor was a great hero. He thought that "SEVEN AT ONE BLOW" meant seven men, not flies.

"There are two terrible giants in our land. We all live in fear of their dreadful deeds," he told the tailor. "If you will kill them for me, I will give you half my kingdom, and my daughter for your wife!"

"Just leave it to me!" said the little tailor, and set off at once. The king sent along a hundred of his best soldiers to help.

When they drew near the place where the giants lived, the little tailor turned to the king's men. "Stay here, out of danger," he said. "I will kill the giants alone!"

The soldiers were very surprised. How could anyone be so brave? But they knew that the tailor had killed SEVEN AT ONE BLOW!

The tailor crept along quietly, looking
all round him for the two giants. At last
he found them — they were asleep under a
tree. Quickly he filled his pockets with the
heaviest stones he could find. Then he
climbed up the tree.

Silently he dropped a stone onto one of the snoring giants, then he dropped one onto the other. They both woke up very angry indeed, each thinking that the other had struck him.

The next moment the giants were fighting. In their anger they ripped up trees and hurled heavy boulders at each other. They fought so hard that they rolled through a forest, flattening all the trees.

On down a hillside they rolled, wrecking barns, fences and haystacks on their way. In fact, they were so busy fighting that they rolled over a cliff edge, down into the sea, and no one ever heard of them again.

The brave little tailor returned to the palace to claim his reward, but the king had two more tasks for him.

"Catch me the unicorn and the wild boar who roam my forest," he ordered. "Only then will I give you half my kingdom and my daughter. Take my huntsmen to help you."

"No sooner said than done!" laughed the tailor, setting out once more. He began to run as fast as he could. Soon he was so far ahead that he was out of sight of the huntsmen.

All at once he heard the unicorn thundering straight at him. Quickly he leapt behind a tree.

The unicorn couldn't stop and his single horn stuck fast in the trunk of the tree. The tailor's cunning had captured him!

The tailor came out from behind the tree, thinking to himself, "How clever I am!"

Then the next moment his delight turned to fear. The wild boar came bounding furiously down the path. The tailor turned and ran for his life.

As he ran, by good chance he spotted a hut in a clearing. He dashed towards it, flung open the door, and leapt sideways out of the way.

The wild boar rushed past him into the hut. Very smartly, the tailor slammed the door — and the boar was trapped!

One by one the king's terrified huntsmen crept out of the forest. Quickly they tied up both animals and led them back to the palace in triumph.

The king was overjoyed. "Take half my kingdom and my daughter. Stay with us, brave little tailor. Our land will always be safe with the man who killed SEVEN AT ONE BLOW!"